4/15 GT 25.00

DOROTHY AND THE WIZARD IN OZ

VOL. 2

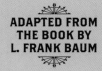

ADAPTED FROM
THE BOOK BY
L. FRANK BAUM

Writer: **ERIC SHANOWER**
Artist: **SKOTTIE YOUNG**
Colorist: **JEAN-FRANCOIS BEAULIEU**
Letterer: **JEFF ECKLEBERRY**

Assistant Editors: **RACHEL PINNELAS & JON MOISAN**
Editor: **SANA AMANAT**

Collection Editor: **MARK D. BEAZLEY**
Assistant Editors: **NELSON RIBEIRO & ALEX STARBUCK**
Editor, Special Projects: **JENNIFER GRÜNWALD**
Senior Editor, Special Projects: **JEFF YOUNGQUIST**
Senior Vice President Print, Sales & Marketing: **DAVID GABRIEL**

Editor in Chief: **AXEL ALONSO**
Chief Creative Officer: **JOE QUESADA**
Publisher: **DAN BUCKLEY**
Executive Producer: **ALAN FINE**

ABDO
Spotlight

ABDOPUBLISHING.COM

Reinforced library bound edition published in 2015 by Spotlight,
a division of ABDO, PO Box 398166, Minneapolis, Minnesota 55439.
Spotlight produces high-quality reinforced library bound editions for
schools and libraries. Published by agreement with Marvel Characters, Inc.

Printed in the United States of America, North Mankato, Minnesota.
112014
012015

THIS BOOK CONTAINS
RECYCLED MATERIALS

Marvel.com
© 2014 Marvel

LIBRARY OF CONGRESS CATALOGING-IN-PUBLICATION DATA

Shanower, Eric.
  Dorothy and the Wizard in Oz / adapted from the novel by L. Frank Baum ;
writer: Eric Shanower ; artist: Skottie Young. -- Reinforced library bound
edition.
      pages cm
  "Marvel."
  Summary: During a California earthquake Dorothy falls into the
underground Land of the Mangaboos where she again meets the Wizard of
Oz.
  ISBN 978-1-61479-343-4 (vol. 1) -- ISBN 978-1-61479-344-1 (vol. 2) -- ISBN
978-1-61479-345-8 (vol. 3) -- ISBN 978-1-61479-346-5 (vol. 4) -- ISBN 978-1-
61479-347-2 (vol. 5) -- ISBN 978-1-61479-348-9 (vol. 6) -- ISBN 978-1-61479-
349-6 (vol. 7) -- ISBN 978-1-61479-350-2 (vol. 8)
  1. Graphic novels. [1. Graphic novels. 2. Fantasy.] I. Young, Skottie,
illustrator. II. Baum, L. Frank (Lyman Frank), 1856-1919. Dorothy and the
Wizard in Oz. III. Title.
  PZ7.7.S453Dor 2015
  741.5'973--dc23
                    2014033625

Spotlight

A Division of ABDO
abdopublishing.com

YES, MY DEAR, I AM OZ--

--THE GREAT AND TERRIBLE, EH?

AND YOU'RE LITTLE DOROTHY FROM KANSAS. I REMEMBER YOU VERY WELL.

WHO DID YOU SAY IT WAS, DOROTHY?

IT'S THE WONDERFUL WIZARD OF OZ, ZEB. HAVEN'T YOU HEARD OF HIM?

SIR, WHY ARE YOU HERE IN THE LAND OF THE MANGA-BOOS?

DIDN'T KNOW WHAT LAND IT WAS, MY SON. TO BE HONEST, I DIDN'T MEAN TO VISIT YOU WHEN I STARTED OUT.

I LIVE ON THE TOP OF THE EARTH, YOUR HONOR, WHICH IS FAR BETTER THAN LIVING INSIDE IT.

"THIS MORNING I WENT UP IN A BALLOON. WHEN I CAME DOWN I FELL INTO A BIG CRACK IN THE EARTH CAUSED BY AN EARTHQUAKE.

"I'D LET SO MUCH GAS OUT OF MY BALLOON THAT I COULDN'T RISE AGAIN. IN A FEW MINUTES THE EARTH CLOSED OVER MY HEAD."

I CONTINUED TO DESCEND UNTIL I REACHED THIS PLACE. IF YOU'LL SHOW ME A WAY OUT, I'LL GO WITH PLEASURE. SORRY TO HAVE TROUBLED YOU, BUT IT COULDN'T BE HELPED.

THIS CHILD CALLED YOU A WIZARD. IS NOT A WIZARD SOMETHING LIKE A SORCERER?

IT'S BETTER! ONE WIZARD IS WORTH *THREE* SORCERERS.

AH, YOU SHALL PROVE THAT! COME WITH ME--I WISH YOU TO MEET OUR SORCERER.

WE MANGABOOS HAVE, AT THE PRESENT TIME, ONE OF THE MOST WONDERFUL SORCERERS THAT EVER WAS PICKED FROM A BUSH--BUT HE SOMETIMES MAKES MISTAKES.

DO *YOU* EVER MAKE MISTAKES?

NEVER!

OH, OZ! YOU MADE A LOT OF MISTAKES WHEN YOU WERE IN THE MARVELOUS LAND OF OZ.

NONSENSE!

WHAT AN ABSURD CREATURE!

HE MAY LOOK ABSURD, BUT HE IS AN EXCELLENT SORCERER. THE ONLY FAULT I FIND WITH HIM IS THAT HE IS SO OFTEN WRONG.

I AM NEVER WRONG!

ONLY A SHORT TIME AGO YOU TOLD ME THERE WOULD BE NO MORE RAIN OF STONES OR OF PEOPLE. HERE IS ANOTHER PERSON DESCENDED FROM THE AIR TO PROVE YOU WERE WRONG.

ONE PERSON CANNOT BE CALLED "PEOPLE."

IF *TWO* SHOULD COME OUT OF THE SKY YOU MIGHT SAY I WAS WRONG. BUT UNLESS MORE THAN ONE APPEARS I WILL HOLD THAT I WAS RIGHT.

VERY CLEVER! I'M DELIGHTED TO FIND HUMBUGS INSIDE THE EARTH, JUST THE SAME AS ON TOP OF IT. YOU OUGHT TO JOIN A CIRCUS, BROTHER.

I BELONG TO BAILUM AND BARNEY'S GREAT CONSOLIDATED SHOWS-- A FINE AGGREGATION, I ASSURE YOU.

I GO UP IN A BALLOON TO DRAW CROWDS TO THE CIRCUS. I'VE JUST HAD THE BAD LUCK TO LAND LOWER DOWN THAN I INTENDED.

BUT NEVER MIND. IT ISN'T EVERYBODY WHO GETS A CHANC[E] TO SEE YOUR LAND OF THE GABA-ZOOS.

MANGABOOS! IF YOU ARE A WIZARD YOU OUGHT TO BE ABLE TO CALL PEOPLE BY THEIR RIGHT NAMES.

OH, I'M A WIZARD--JUST AS GOOD A WIZARD AS YOU ARE A SORCERER.

IF YOU ARE ABLE TO PROVE THAT YOU ARE BETTER, I'LL MAKE YOU THE CHIEF WIZARD OF THIS DOMAIN. OTHERWISE, I'LL STOP YOU FROM LIVING AND FORBID YOU TO BE PLANTED.

THAT DOESN'T SOUND ESPECIALLY PLEASANT. BUT NEVER MIND. I'LL BEAT OLD PRICKLY, ALL RIGHT.

MY NAME IS GWIG! LET ME SEE YOU EQUAL THE SORCERY I AM ABOUT TO PERFORM.

I HEAR BELLS TINKLING, BUT--

THERE ARE NO BELLS AT ALL!

THE WIZARD CAUGHT THE PIGLET...

...AND HOLDING ITS HEAD IN ONE HAND AND ITS TAIL IN THE OTHER, HE PULLED IT APART AND--

THE WIZARD CONTINUED UNTIL NINE TINY PIGLETS WERE DISPLAYED.

SQUEE!

NOW, HAVING CREATED SOMETHING FROM NOTHING, I WILL MAKE SOMETHING NOTHING AGAIN.

SQUEE!

GRUNT!

ONE BY ONE THE PIGLETS WERE PUSHED TOGETHER UNTIL BUT A SINGLE ONE REMAINED.

SQUEE!

YOU ARE INDEED A WONDERFUL WIZARD, AND YOUR POWERS ARE GREATER THAN THOSE OF MY SORCERER.

HE WILL NOT BE A WONDERFUL WIZARD LONG.

WHY NOT?

BECAUSE I AM GOING TO STOP YOUR BREATH. I PERCEIVE THAT YOU ARE CURIOUSLY CONSTRUCTED, AND THAT IF YOU CANNOT BREATHE YOU CANNOT KEEP ALIVE.

IT WILL TAKE ABOUT FIVE MINUTES. WATCH ME CAREFULLY.

*B*UT THE WIZARD DIDN'T WATCH. HE DREW A LEATHER CASE FROM HIS POCKET.

HUHH-- GAAAH--

UHHH-- KHHUUH-- *HUUUU*--

AAAAH!

HAH!

WHY, HE'S VEGETABLE!

OF COURSE. WE ARE ALL VEGETABLE IN THIS COUNTRY. ARE YOU NOT VEGETABLE ALSO?

NO, PEOPLE ON TOP OF THE EARTH ARE ALL MEAT.

HE IS DEAD AND WILL WITHER QUICKLY. WE MUST PLANT HIM AT ONCE. IF YOU WILL ACCOMPANY ME, I WILL EXPLAIN THE MYSTERIES OF OUR VEGETABLE KINGDOM.

*T*HEY PASSED THROUGH THE STREETS OF THE GLASS CITY TO A BROAD PLAIN.

THESE ARE OUR PUBLIC GARDENS.

WHO BUILT THOSE LOVELY BRIDGES?

NO ONE BUILT THEM. THEY GROW.

THAT'S STRANGE. DID THE GLASS HOUSES IN YOUR CITY GROW, TOO?

OF COURSE. BUT IT TOOK A GOOD MANY YEARS. THAT IS WHY WE ARE SO ANGRY WHEN A RAIN OF STONES COMES TO BREAK OUR TOWERS AND CRACK OUR ROOFS.

CAN'T YOU MEND THEM?

NO. BUT THEY WILL GROW TOGETHER AGAIN IN TIME. WE MUST WAIT UNTIL THEY DO.

A NICE COUNTRY THIS IS-- WHERE A RESPECTABLE HORSE HAS TO EAT PINK GRASS!

IT'S VIOLET.

NOW IT'S BLUE. AS A MATTER OF FACT, I'M EATING RAINBOW GRASS.

HOW DOES IT TASTE?

NOT BAD AT ALL. IF THEY GIVE ME PLENTY OF IT, I WON'T COMPLAIN ABOUT ITS COLOR.

THIS IS OUR PLANTING GROUND.

THE SORCERER WILL SPROUT SOON AND GROW INTO A LARGE BUSH FROM WHICH WE SHALL IN TIME BE ABLE TO PICK SEVERAL VERY GOOD SORCERERS.

DO ALL YOUR PEOPLE GROW ON BUSHES?

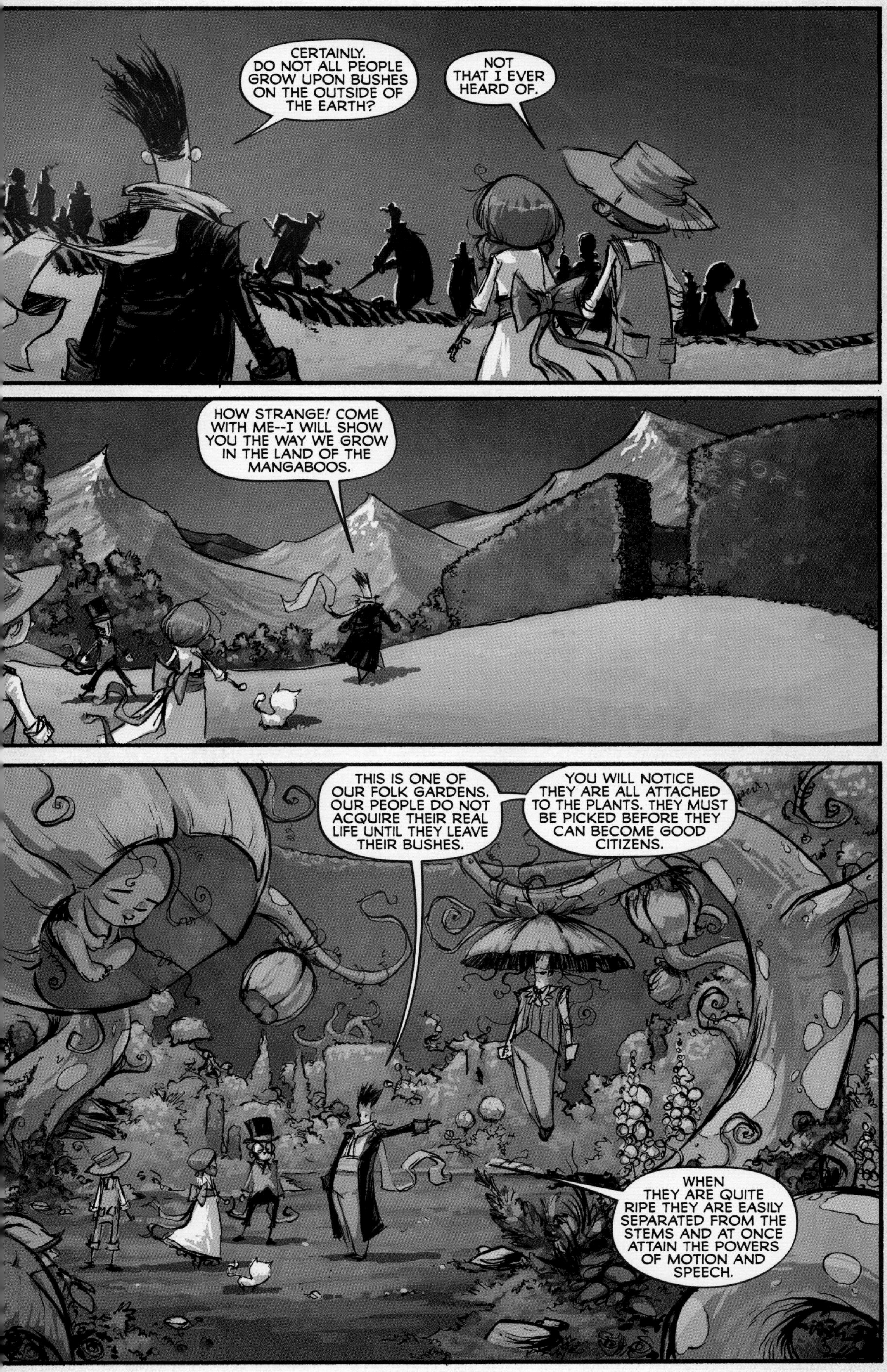
CERTAINLY. DO NOT ALL PEOPLE GROW UPON BUSHES ON THE OUTSIDE OF THE EARTH?
NOT THAT I EVER HEARD OF.
HOW STRANGE! COME WITH ME--I WILL SHOW YOU THE WAY WE GROW IN THE LAND OF THE MANGABOOS.
THIS IS ONE OF OUR FOLK GARDENS. OUR PEOPLE DO NOT ACQUIRE THEIR REAL LIFE UNTIL THEY LEAVE THEIR BUSHES.
YOU WILL NOTICE THEY ARE ALL ATTACHED TO THE PLANTS. THEY MUST BE PICKED BEFORE THEY CAN BECOME GOOD CITIZENS.
WHEN THEY ARE QUITE RIPE THEY ARE EASILY SEPARATED FROM THE STEMS AND AT ONCE ATTAIN THE POWERS OF MOTION AND SPEECH.

HOW LONG DO YOU LIVE AFTER YOU'RE PICKED?

IF WE KEEP COOL AND MOIST AND MEET WITH NO ACCIDENTS, WE OFTEN LIVE FOR FIVE YEARS. I'VE BEEN PICKED OVER SIX YEARS, BUT OUR FAMILY IS KNOWN TO BE ESPECIALLY LONG-LIVED.

DO YOU EAT?

EAT! NO, INDEED. WE ARE QUITE SOLID INSIDE, AND HAVE NO NEED TO EAT, ANY MORE THAN DOES A POTATO.

THIS IS THE ROYAL BUSH OF THE MANGABOOS. ALL OF OUR RULERS HAVE GROWN UPON THIS ONE BUSH FROM TIME IMMEMORIAL.

BUT POTATOES SOMETIMES SPROUT!

AND SOMETIMES WE DO--BUT THAT IS CONSIDERED A GREAT MISFORTUNE, FOR THEN WE MUST BE PLANTED AT ONCE.

WHERE DID *YOU* GROW?

I WILL SHOW YOU. STEP THIS WAY, PLEASE.

WHO IS THIS?

SHE IS THE ROYAL PRINCESS DESTINED TO BE MY SUCCESSOR. WHEN SHE BECOMES FULLY RIPE I MUST ABANDON THE SOVEREIGNTY OF THE MANGABOOS TO HER.

ISN'T SHE RIPE NOW?

NOT *QUITE.*

IT WILL BE SEVERAL DAYS BEFORE SHE NEEDS TO BE PICKED--OR AT LEAST THAT IS MY JUDGMENT.

I AM IN NO HURRY TO RESIGN MY OFFICE AND BE PLANTED, YOU MAY BE SURE.

PROBABLY NOT.

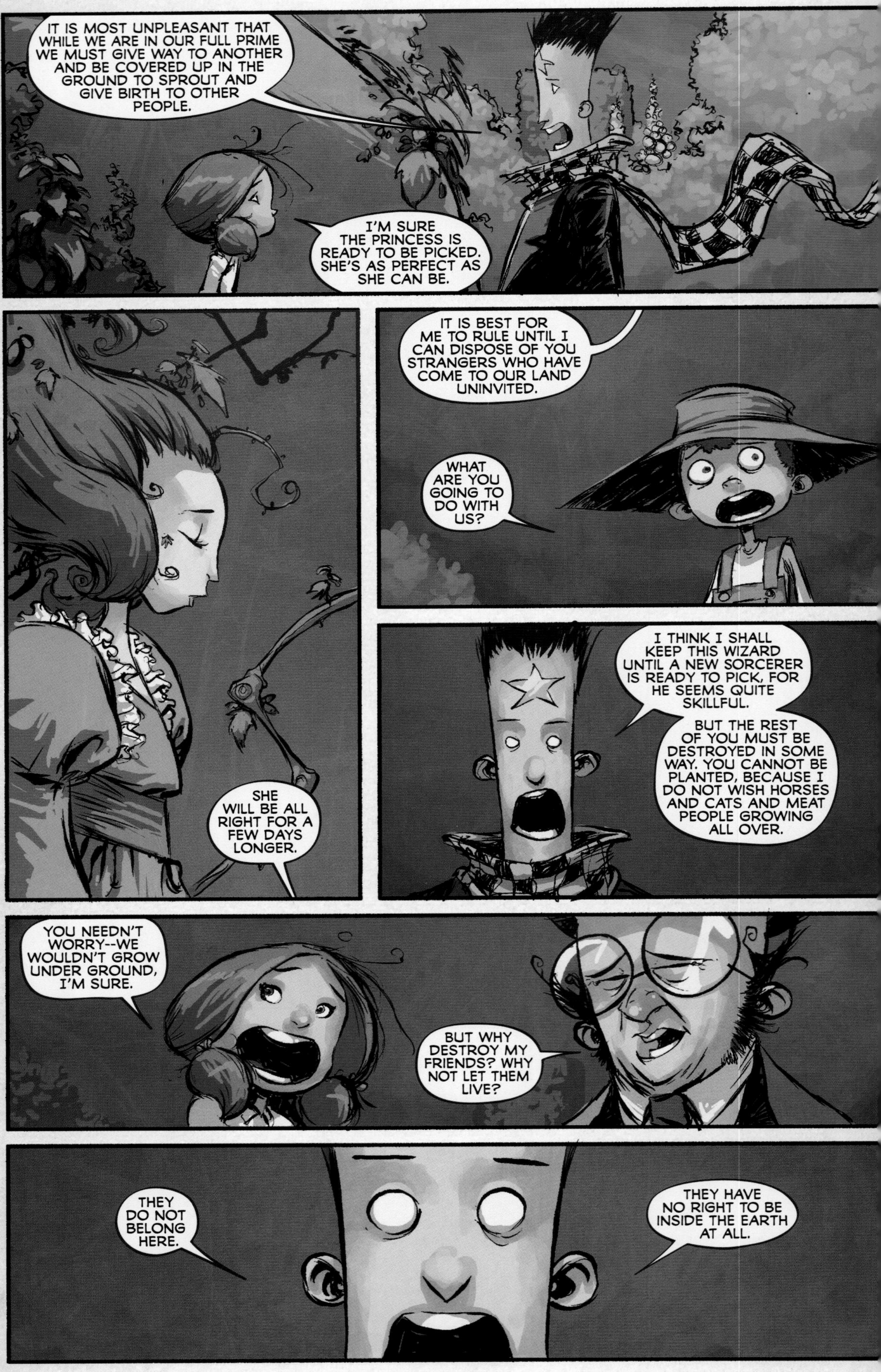
IT IS MOST UNPLEASANT THAT WHILE WE ARE IN OUR FULL PRIME WE MUST GIVE WAY TO ANOTHER AND BE COVERED UP IN THE GROUND TO SPROUT AND GIVE BIRTH TO OTHER PEOPLE.
I'M SURE THE PRINCESS IS READY TO BE PICKED. SHE'S AS PERFECT AS SHE CAN BE.
SHE WILL BE ALL RIGHT FOR A FEW DAYS LONGER.
IT IS BEST FOR ME TO RULE UNTIL I CAN DISPOSE OF YOU STRANGERS WHO HAVE COME TO OUR LAND UNINVITED.
WHAT ARE YOU GOING TO DO WITH US?
I THINK I SHALL KEEP THIS WIZARD UNTIL A NEW SORCERER IS READY TO PICK, FOR HE SEEMS QUITE SKILLFUL.
BUT THE REST OF YOU MUST BE DESTROYED IN SOME WAY. YOU CANNOT BE PLANTED, BECAUSE I DO NOT WISH HORSES AND CATS AND MEAT PEOPLE GROWING ALL OVER.
YOU NEEDN'T WORRY--WE WOULDN'T GROW UNDER GROUND, I'M SURE.
BUT WHY DESTROY MY FRIENDS? WHY NOT LET THEM LIVE?
THEY DO NOT BELONG HERE.
THEY HAVE NO RIGHT TO BE INSIDE THE EARTH AT ALL.

WE DIDN'T ASK TO COME DOWN HERE--WE FELL!

THAT IS NO EXCUSE.

HE WON'T NEED TO DESTROY *ME*--IF I DON'T GET SOMETHING TO EAT PRETTY SOON I'LL STARVE TO DEATH AND SAVE HIM THE TROUBLE.

IF HE PLANTED YOU, HE MIGHT GROW SOME CATTAILS.

PERHAPS WE CAN FIND YOU SOME MILKWEEDS TO EAT.

PHOO! I WOULDN'T TOUCH THE NASTY THINGS!

I'M HUNGRY MYSELF. I NOTICED SOME STRAWBERRIES GROWING IN ONE OF THE GARDENS AND SOME MELONS IN ANOTHER PLACE.

NEVER MIND YOUR HUNGER. I SHALL ORDER YOU DESTROYED IN A FEW MINUTES, SO YOU WILL HAVE NO NEED TO RUIN OUR PRETTY MELON VINES AND BERRY BUSHES.

FOLLOW ME, PLEASE, TO MEET YOUR DOOM.

WAIT!

WHAT FOR?

SUPPOSE WE PICK THE ROYAL PRINCESS--I'M QUITE SURE SHE'S RIPE. AS SOON AS SHE COMES TO LIFE SHE'LL BE THE RULER AND MAY TREAT US BETTER THAN THAT HEARTLESS PRINCE.

ALL RIGHT!

LET'S PICK HER WHILE WE HAVE THE CHANCE, BEFORE THE MAN WITH THE STAR COMES BACK.

PULL!

OHHHHH... I THANK YOU VERY MUCH.

WE SALUTE YOUR ROYAL HIGHNESS!

FOLLOW ME AT ONCE! MAKE HASTE AND--*OH!*

SIR, YOU HAVE WRONGED ME GREATLY, AND WOULD HAVE WRONGED ME STILL MORE HAD NOT THESE STRANGERS COME TO MY RESCUE.

I HAVE BEEN READY FOR PICKING ALL THE PAST WEEK, BUT BECAUSE YOU WERE SELFISH AND DESIRED TO CONTINUE YOUR UNLAWFUL RULE, YOU LEFT ME TO STAND SILENT UPON MY BUSH.

I DID NOT KNOW THAT YOU WERE RIPE.

GIVE ME THE STAR OF ROYALTY!

*T*HE PRINCE TOOK THE STAR FROM HIS BROW AND PLACED IT ON THAT OF THE PRINCESS, THEN BOWED.

WHAT BECAME OF THE MANGABOO PRINCE AFTERWARD OUR FRIENDS NEVER KNEW.

THE PEOPLE ESCORTED THEIR NEW RULER TO HER PALACE.

NO ONE SEEMED TO PAY ANY ATTENTION TO DOROTHY AND HER FRIENDS.

I WONDER WHY WE CAN WALK SO EASILY IN THE AIR.

PERHAPS IT'S BECAUSE WE'RE CLOSE TO THE CENTER OF THE EARTH, WHERE THE ATTRACTION OF GRAVITATION IS SLIGHT. MANY ODD THINGS HAPPEN IN FAIRY COUNTRIES.

IS THIS A FAIRY COUNTRY?

OF COURSE IT IS-- ONLY A FAIRY COUNTRY COULD HAVE VEGETABLE PEOPLE. AND ONLY IN A FAIRY COUNTRY COULD EUREKA AND JIM TALK.

GIVE ME MILK--OR MEAT! YOU--WIZARD-- WHY CAN'T YOU BRING ME A DISH OF MILK BY MEANS OF YOUR MAGICAL ARTS? I DON'T BELIEVE YOU'RE A WIZARD AT ALL!

YOU'RE QUITE RIGHT. IN THE STRICT SENSE OF THE WORD I'M NOT A WIZARD, BUT ONLY A HUMBUG.

IF THAT'S SO, HOW COULD YOU DO THAT WONDERFUL TRICK WITH THE NINE TINY PIGLETS?

IT MUST HAVE BEEN HUMBUG. THE WIZARD OF OZ HAS ALWAYS BEEN A HUMBUG.

VERY TRUE. IT WAS NECESSARY TO DECEIVE THAT UGLY SORCERER AND THE PRINCE--BUT THE THING WAS ONLY A TRICK.

BUT I SAW THE LITTLE PIGS WITH MY OWN EYES!

SO DID I!

TO BE SURE--YOU SAW THEM BECAUSE THEY WERE THERE. BUT PULLING THEM APART AND PUSHING THEM TOGETHER WAS ONLY A SLEIGHT-OF-HAND TRICK.

THEY'RE IN MY POCKET NOW.

HERE THEY ARE! THEY'RE HUNGRY, TOO.

SQUEE!

GRUNT-GRUNT!

OH, WHAT CUNNING THINGS!

BE CAREFUL! YOU'RE SQUEEZING ME!

MAY I EAT ONE? I'M AWFULLY HUNGRY.

WHY, EUREKA! WHAT A CRUEL QUESTION! IT WOULD BE DREADFUL TO EAT THESE DEAR LITTLE THINGS.

I SHOULD SAY SO!

CATS ARE CRUEL THINGS!

I'M NOT CRUEL--

--I'M JUST HUNGRY.

YOU CANNOT EAT MY PIGLETS, EVEN IF YOU'RE STARVING. THEY'RE THE ONLY THINGS I HAVE TO PROVE I'M A WIZARD.

I NEVER SAW SUCH SMALL PIGS BEFORE.

"THEY'RE FROM THE ISLAND OF TEENTY-WEENT, WHERE EVERYTHING IS SMALL. A SAILOR BROUGHT THEM TO LOS ANGELES AND I GAVE HIM NINE TICKETS TO THE CIRCUS FOR THEM."

BUT WHAT AM I GOING TO EAT? THERE ARE NO COWS TO GIVE MILK, OR MICE, OR EVEN GRASSHOPPERS. YOU MAY AS WELL PLANT ME AND RAISE CATSUP.

I HAVE AN IDEA THAT THERE ARE FISHES IN THESE BROOKS. DO YOU LIKE FISH?

DO I LIKE FISH? WHY, THEY'RE BETTER THAN PIGLETS--OR EVEN MILK!

THE WIZARD BENT A PIN FOR A HOOK AND, WITH A BLOSSOM FOR BAIT, THREW THE END OF HIS LINE IN THE WATER.

SOON.

OH, EUREKA! DID YOU EAT THE BONES? YOU WERE VERY GREEDY.

I WAS VERY HUNGRY! I DON'T THINK THAT FISH HAD ANY BONES, BECAUSE I DIDN'T FEEL THEM SCRATCH MY THROAT.

CATS ARE DREADFUL CREATURES!

I'M GLAD WE ARE NOT FISHES!

LET'S GO BACK TO THE CITY--THAT IS, IF JIM'S HAD ENOUGH OF THE PINK GRASS.

DON'T WORRY--I WON'T LET THE KITTEN HURT YOU.

I'VE TRIED TO EAT A LOT WHILE I HAD THE CHANCE, FOR IT'S LIKELY TO BE A LONG WHILE BETWEEN MEALS IN THIS STRANGE COUNTRY. BUT I'M READY TO GO ANYTIME YOU WISH.

WHERE SHALL WE STAY?

I'LL TAKE POSSESSION OF THE HOUSE OF THE SORCERER. THE PRINCE SAID HE'D KEEP ME UNTIL THEY PICKED ANOTHER SORCERER, AND THE PRINCESS WON'T KNOW BUT THAT WE BELONG THERE.

LOOK DOWN!
THOSE VINES--LIKE A NEST OF GREAT SNAKES!
THEY'RE ALL TWISTING AND WRITHING!
CRUNCH!
I'M THANKFUL TO HAVE ESCAPED ACCIDENTALLY STROLLING AMONG *THEM!*

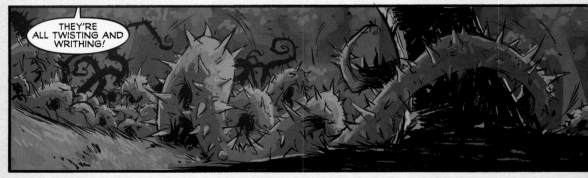

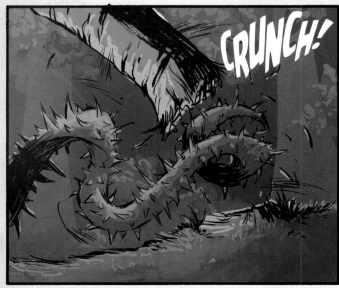